# Lily and the Bee

By:
## Dana R. Brown

# DEDICATION

My daughter, Lily Ann Grace Warner, you are a bright star in this universe. Everything that is good and pure is you. I love you more than you could ever possibly know.

## ACKNOWLEDGMENTS

My Great-Aunt "Bee" has been the biggest influence in my life and made me the person I am today. She has taught me that unconditional love knows no bounds and the world definitely needs more of it.

There once was a bear,
that came upon a bee. . .

You are so tiny!
You don't look a thing like me.

My name is Lily.
We, brown bears, are large and furry.

I like you, little bee.
Let's go on a journey!

Saying hello is a way to be kind.
Say hi to all of the animals that we find!

Some may be BIG!
And some may be small.

Some have eight eyes
and some might have claws.

Some friends may swim
and others might fly!

Friends that run fast
or sleep the day going by.

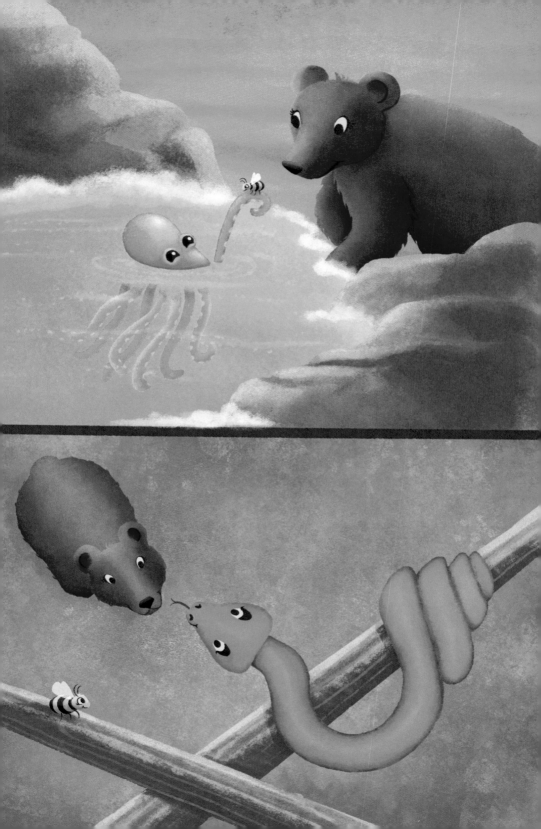

Some have many legs
or some have none at all!

Being tiny is as great
as the friends who are tall!

Some say quack!
And friends that go moo!

Some can lay eggs.
These are the barnyard crew!

Some have horns on their head
or horns on their nose.

Some friends have no horns at all
but fingers and toes!
Wiggle them so everyone knows!

Friends can be green, purple, or blue. . .

But I am lucky to have the one
and only you!

Buzzing around helping each little flower,
spreading the pollen is your superpower!

While I love honey from your hive,
my little bee. . .

I love you even more because you look nothing like me.


The End

## FROM THE AUTHOR

This is my debut children's book. My focus is to create more children's books that center on a message of positivity, inclusion, and environmental health. Noah and the Crab will be next in the series featuring a Puffin named Noah who meets a little crab. Their adventures on the beach will teach lessons of recycling and littering awareness while being the perfect bedtime story for the early reader.

Made in the USA
Columbia, SC
31 March 2021